Who Moved My Cheese?
My Cheese?

An A-Mazing Way to Change and Win! for **Kids**

By the #1 Bestselling Author **SPENCER JOHNSON, M.D.**
and **CHRISTIAN JOHNSON**

ILLUSTRATIONS BY STEVE PILEGGI

G. P. Putnam's Sons   New York

This book is dedicated to my son
Christian Johnson
who contributed so much
to this edition of the story.

Library of Congress Cataloging-in-Publication Data
Johnson, Spencer.   Who moved my cheese? for kids : an a-mazing way to change and win! /
by Spencer Johnson ; illustrations by Steve Pileggi.   p. cm.   Summary: Four little friends in a maze
find and enjoy some cheese, but when that cheese is gone, only Sniff and Scurry adapt and go searching
for more while Hem and Haw wait for more cheese to appear. Includes a note to parents and discussion questions.
[1. Mice—Fiction. 2. Maze puzzles—Fiction. 3. Change—Fiction.] I. Pileggi, Steve, ill. II. Title.
PZ7.J6383 Wh 2003   [E]—dc21   2002151749   ISBN 978-0-399-24016-4
11

To learn more, visit:
www.WhoMovedMyCheese.com

A NOTE TO PARENTS
About Who Moved My Cheese?
for Kids

from
Dr. Spencer
Johnson

Many of the millions of people all around the world who have read *Who Moved My Cheese?* say the same thing: They wish they had known "The Cheese Story" when they were younger. Wouldn't it be great if, as kids, we had known how to deal with change—and win!

Some years ago, our family moved over five thousand miles to a place with a different culture. A few months after the boys began at a new school, their teachers marveled at how well they had adapted.

They had grown up on the story of *Who Moved My Cheese?* and saw that change could be fun and that it could bring them something better. This story really *can* help kids change and win!

Your family may be experiencing many different kinds of change. But whatever it is, we hope your children will enjoy this kids' edition of the story, which has been created especially for them, and that you will all find your own New Cheese—and enjoy it!

Spencer Johnson

Once upon a time, there lived four little friends named Sniff, Scurry, Hem, and Haw.

Every morning they put on their running shoes and got ready to look for what made them happy—*Magical Cheese!*

Magical Cheese was special because when you found it, it made you feel good about yourself!

It was hidden somewhere in a big Maze, where there were many different places to go.

Sniff and Scurry were very smart and always remembered where they had been before. So they kept exploring in *new* places where the Cheese might be.

Sniff had a great nose. He could sniff the air and smell where the Cheese was. Scurry had fast feet. He could scurry ahead and get to the Cheese quickly.

Hem and Haw were also smart. They read books and studied maps to find the Magical Cheese.

"Let's try going this way," Haw would say.

"I'm not so sure," Hem would answer.

Hem and Haw did not want to get lost in any dark corners, so they went through the Maze slowly, one step at a time.

Day after day, the four friends searched through the large Maze to find the Cheese.

They went into dark areas and ran into dead ends. But then they just turned around and headed off in a new direction.

Then, all of a sudden, one lucky day, it happened. All four friends found something wonderful.

What do you think it was?

CHEESE STATION C

They found MAGICAL CHEESE!

It was inside one of the large rooms called Cheese Station C.

It had been there all the time, just waiting for someone to find it.

"Whoopee!" cried Haw.

"Hooray!" yelled Sniff and Scurry.

Hem shouted, "There's enough here to last us all *forever!*"

Sniff liked the orange slices that smelled nice. Scurry nibbled on the hard yellow cubes of Cheese. Hem liked the kind with holes in it. And Haw enjoyed the soft white Cheese, shaped like a wheel.

Each began to imagine what the Magical Cheese could bring them.

Sniff pictured himself playing with new friends at Blue Cheese Park. Scurry imagined himself scoring the winning goal in Cheese soccer. Haw saw himself getting good grades at Brie Elementary School. And Hem dreamed he lived in a great home atop Swiss Cheese Hill. Later, as night fell, they all headed toward their little houses.

The next morning, Sniff and Scurry woke up early and laced up their running shoes.
They raced through the Maze, straight to Cheese Station C.

When they got there, Sniff smelled the Cheese to see if it was still fresh, and Scurry measured it to see how much was left.

When they were satisfied there was enough Cheese for another day, they took off their running shoes and hung them around their necks so they could find them quickly if they needed them again.

Then, Sniff and Scurry settled in and began to enjoy the Magical Cheese.

Meanwhile, Hem and Haw slept later and later.

"We already know where the Cheese is," Hem thought. "I don't need to hurry."

Haw yawned. "It's comfortable here in my bed. I'll just sleep a little more."

When Hem and Haw finally arrived at Cheese Station C, they made themselves right at home. Hem built himself a Cheese chair to relax in. Haw wrote on the wall: *HAVING CHEESE MAKES YOU HAPPY.*

CHEESE STATION C

Day after day, Sniff and Scurry got up early, scurried over to Cheese Station C, and measured the Cheese to see what was happening.

But Hem and Haw slept later and later every day. They did not pay much attention to the Cheese. They just expected it to always be there.

Can you see what was happening to the Cheese?

Then one morning, Sniff and Scurry arrived early at Cheese Station C to find that the Cheese was gone!

They were not completely surprised since they had noticed the supply of Cheese had been getting smaller.

They knew that they were going to have to go back into the Maze to look for New Cheese.

"I bet it will be just as good as the Old Cheese!" said Scurry.

"Even better," said Sniff. He squealed, "The New Cheese will be even *better!*"

Much later, Hem and Haw arrived at empty Cheese Station C. They looked around. They could not believe their eyes!

Hem yelled, "What! No Cheese? No Cheese? Who moved my Cheese?"

Hem got very angry. He thought the Cheese would always be his—something he deserved to have, no matter what. He jumped up and down, shouting, "IT'S NOT FAIR!"

Haw was just as disappointed as Hem, but he did not yell or stamp his feet.
Haw stood perfectly still, like a statue. He did not know what to do. He was shocked!
Then Haw noticed something. "Hem," he said. "Where are Sniff and Scurry?"

Hem looked around. "I don't know," he answered.

"I bet they went back into the Maze to find New Cheese," said Haw. "Maybe we should too."

"No," said Hem. "I don't want to. It's too confusing out there in the Maze. Remember how hard it was to find *this* Cheese? It's safer to just wait until they put the Old Cheese back here again."

Haw listened to his friend and he became afraid too. "I guess you're right, Hem," Haw said.

CHEESE
STATION C

The next day, Hem and Haw went back to empty Cheese Station C. They were hoping the Cheese would come back.

Every day, they waited . . . and waited . . . and waited, hoping for everything to be just like it was before.

Meanwhile, Sniff and Scurry were sniffing and scurrying through the Maze, looking for New Cheese.

Some days they found little bits of Magical Cheese and stopped for a quick snack. They always left some behind for their friends Hem and Haw.

Then they found a new area of the Maze! It was called Cheese Station N!
The Cheese supply was TEN TIMES bigger than back at Cheese Station C!

But Hem and Haw were still waiting back at empty Cheese Station C.

Finally, Haw looked at his friend and started laughing. "Haw, Haw. Look at us. We look funny. Things have changed, but *we* haven't changed."

Hem was too mad to laugh.

But when Haw laughed at himself, he felt better.

Then Haw wrote on the wall: *WHAT WOULD YOU DO IF YOU WEREN'T AFRAID?*

Haw knew. "Let's go into the Maze, Hem."

But Hem said, "No. I don't want to."

For a change, Haw did not listen to Hem. He said, "It's time to change and find New Magical Cheese!"

What Would You Do

If You Weren't Afraid?

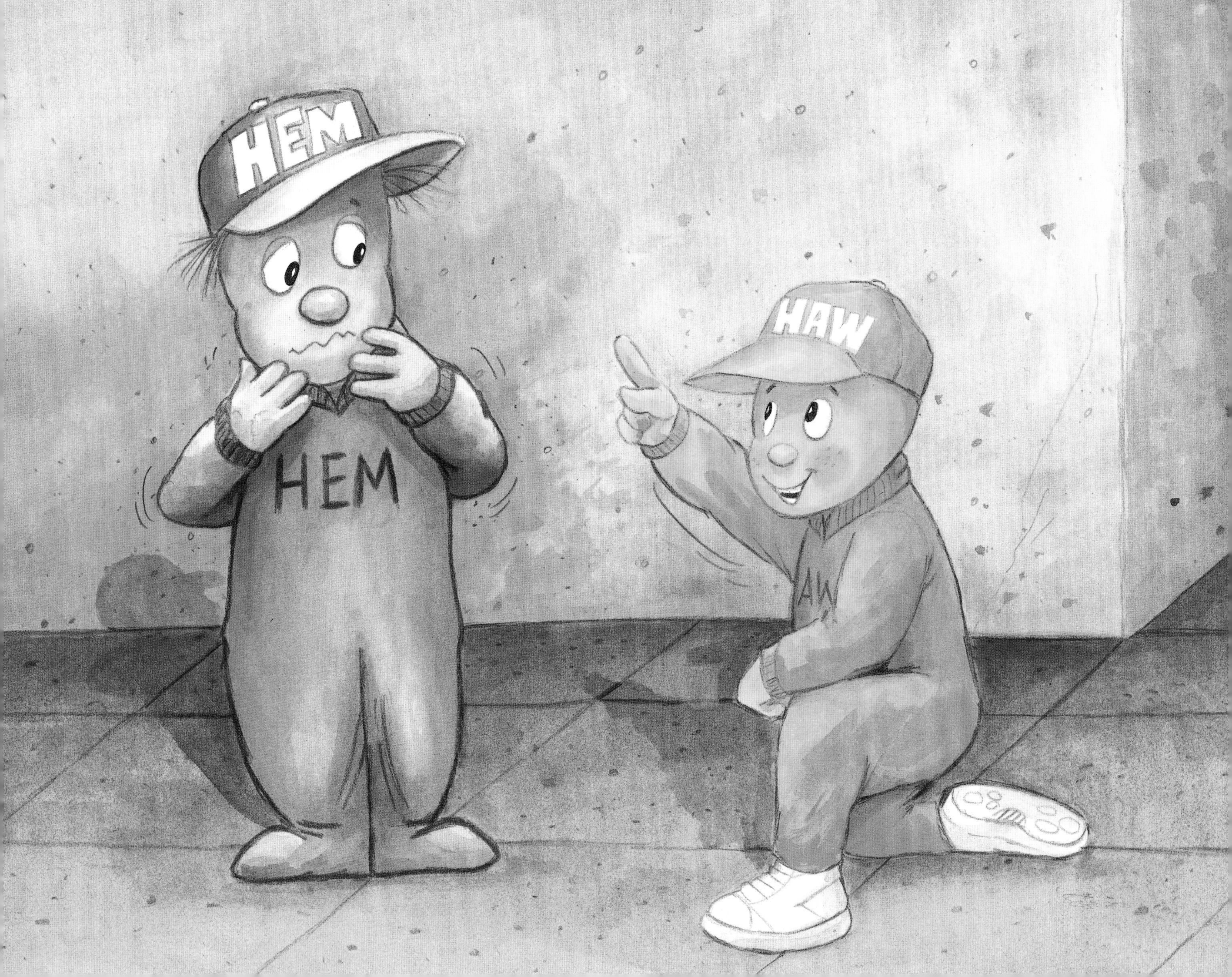

Haw shouted, "It's Maze time!" and ran into the Maze.

At first, Haw was nervous because he did not know what was going to happen.

But the more Haw thought about how much he would enjoy New Magical Cheese, the more confident he became. He felt free. He wondered, "Why do I feel so good?"

Haw realized it was because he was not so afraid. He wrote on the wall: *WHEN YOU STOP BEING AFRAID, YOU FEEL GOOD!*

Haw hoped that Hem might come along and read the "handwriting on the wall." Haw even drew arrows to show which way he was going.

Then he ran on into the Maze! And there, around a corner, he came upon Cheese Station E and he found . . .

CHEESE STATION E

The Sooner You Let Go
of Old Cheese,
The Sooner You Find
New Cheese!

. . . nothing!

Cheese Station E was empty except for a few bits of Cheese.

"I bet there used to be more Cheese here. But Sniff and Scurry probably ate it," Haw said. "If I had just changed faster, I could have shared it with them."

He went over and wrote on the wall of Cheese Station E: *THE SOONER YOU LET GO OF OLD CHEESE, THE SOONER YOU FIND NEW CHEESE!*

As Haw went into new areas of the Maze, he found more and more bits of Magical Cheese. It did not taste anything like the Old Cheese he was used to. Haw was surprised. "It tastes *better!* I'll go back and tell Hem about this."

So he went back through the Maze, all the way back to his friend in Cheese Station C.

When Haw arrived, he found Hem lying on the floor. "Hem!" he cried. "Hem!"

Hem said weakly, "Haw. I am so glad to see you. It's lonely here. Did you find more Cheese out there? The kind I like, with the holes in it?"

"Well, no," said Haw. "But I did find a few bits of New Magical Cheese. It's really good. Here, try some."

"Oh, no," said Hem. "I don't think I would like it. I'll just wait until they put my Old Cheese back."

"Hem, the Old Cheese is gone," said Haw. "It's time for us to find New Cheese. I know it seems scary at first, but once you get going, it's fun!"

"No," said Hem stubbornly.

So, sadly, Haw waved good-bye and went back into the Maze.

Haw was sad because his friend would not change.

But he was not going to stay in empty Cheese Station C, feeling sorry for himself.

He wanted to explore the Maze as he really believed he could find New Cheese.

Soon, Haw raced along and exclaimed, "Aha! I feel good because I have changed. I'm doing something new. It's fun! I like the new me."

Then, Haw entered the darkest part of the Maze.

To help him find his way, Haw imagined his New Magical Cheese. He pictured himself finding and enjoying his New Magical Cheese. He felt better and better!

Haw thought, "Seeing this picture is like having a dream, even while I am wide-awake. It seems so *real!*"

What do you think *your* New Cheese could be?

Imagining Your New Cheese
Helps You Find It!

The more Haw imagined himself finding something *better*, the easier it was for him to find his way.

He stopped and wrote on the wall: *IMAGINING YOUR NEW CHEESE HELPS YOU FIND IT!*

When Haw moved on, he found himself in a part of the Maze with new smells and new colors. It was brighter and welcoming. Then Haw rounded the corner and was absolutely a-mazed at what he saw.

Can you guess what it was?

Right in front of Haw was Cheese Station N!

"Wow! Look at all this New Magical Cheese!" Haw exclaimed.

He dove right into it, just like he had imagined.

Then he shouted, "This *is* better than the Old Cheese!"

CHEESE STATION N

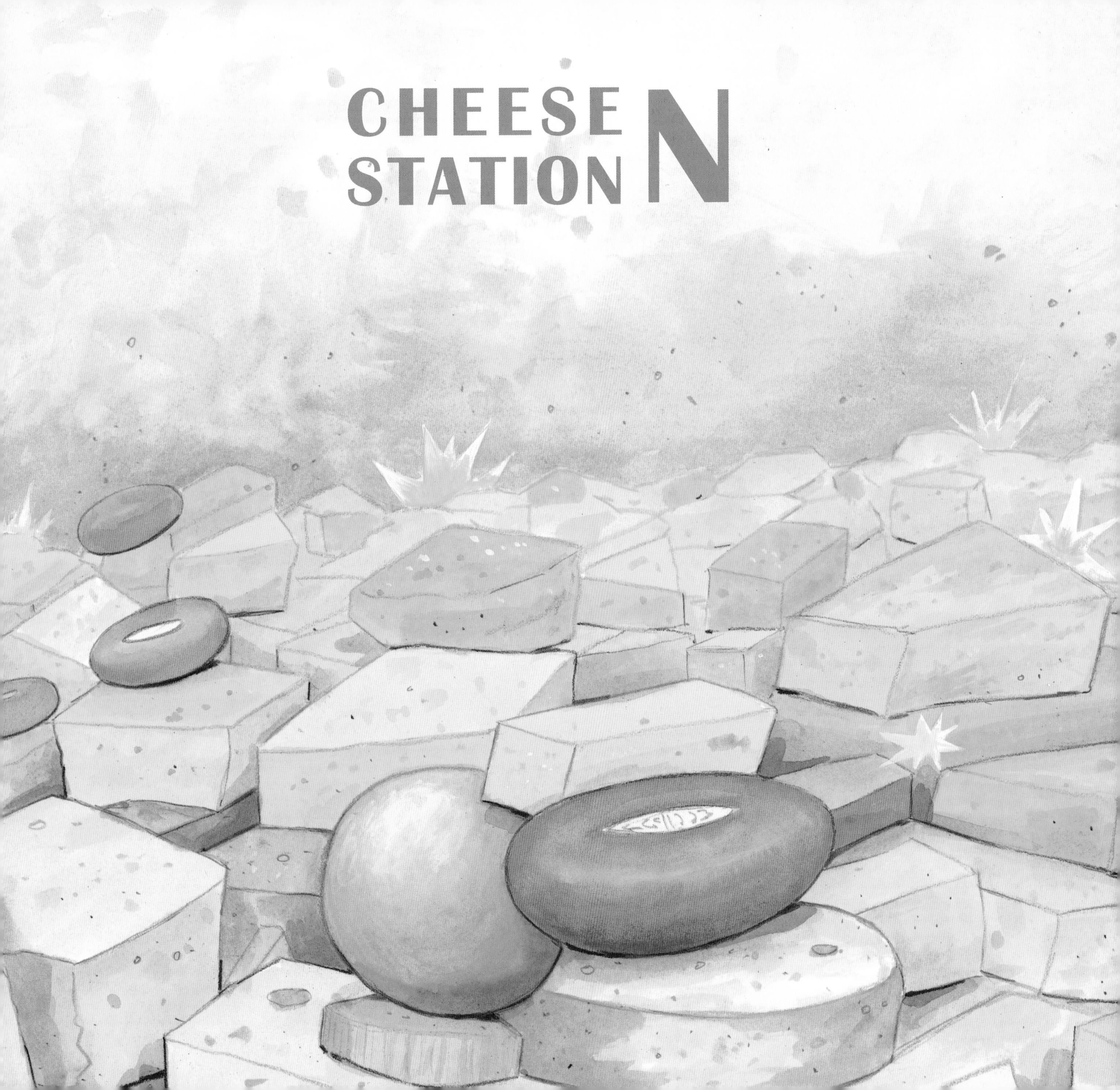

Haw's dream had come true! He was so happy!
Then he heard the sound of laughter.

Haw looked over and saw Sniff and Scurry, who were so glad that Haw had arrived. Haw realized, "I should have moved to the New Cheese sooner, the way Sniff and Scurry did."

Haw helped Scurry measure the Cheese to see how much was really there.
"From now on, I am going to pay attention to what is happening with the Cheese."
Then he wrote on the wall: *SMELL THE CHEESE OFTEN SO YOU KNOW WHEN IT IS
GETTING OLD.*

Smell The Cheese Often So You Know
When It Is Getting Old.

Later, Haw thought about his journey through the Maze. He had learned a lot!

It seemed like only yesterday he believed change happened *to* him—like when someone moved his Cheese from Cheese Station C. Now he realized that the best change happens *inside* of you—like when you believe a change can lead to something better.

After thinking about his time in the Maze, he wrote on the wall what he had learned:

THE HANDWRITING ON THE WALL

Having Cheese Makes You Happy.

What Would You Do
If You Weren't Afraid?

When You Stop Being Afraid,
You Feel Good!

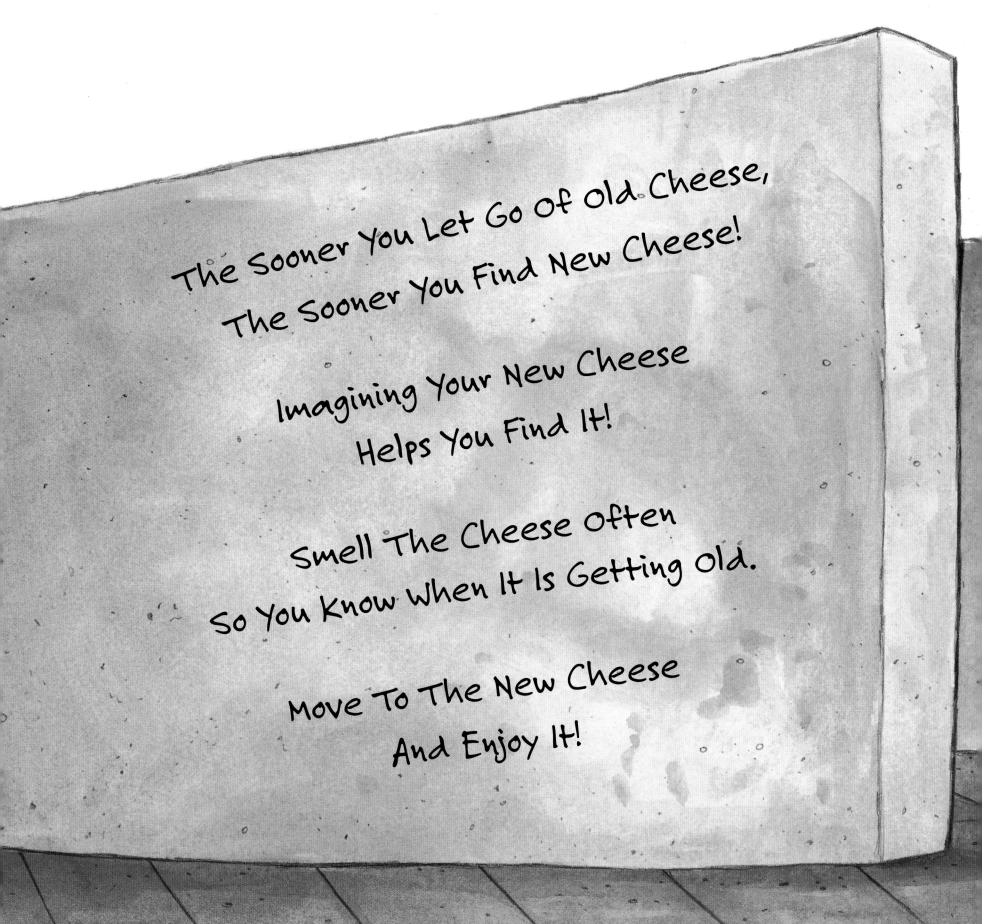

All of a sudden, Haw thought he heard a sound somewhere in the Maze.

Was someone coming? Had Hem read the handwriting on the wall and found his way?

Haw turned his head, and crossed his fingers for good luck. He hoped with all his might that maybe his friend was finally able to . . .

Move To The New Cheese And Enjoy It!

The End

A DISCUSSION

Now that you know the Story of *Who Moved My Cheese? for Kids*, what do you think?

- Do you think Hem changed?
- Are you like Sniff, Scurry, Hem, or Haw?
- Could Haw change his friend Hem? Or can you only change yourself?
- What do you do when your Cheese is moved?
- What could your New Magical Cheese be?
- How could you do something new to change and win today?